Dear Parents:

Congratulations! Your child is taking the first steps on an exciting journey. The destination? Independent reading!

STEP INTO READING® will help your child get there. The program offers five steps to reading success. Each step includes fun stories and colorful art or photographs. In addition to original fiction and books with favorite characters, there are Step into Reading Non-Fiction Readers, Phonics Readers and Boxed Sets, Sticker Readers, and Comic Readers—a complete literacy program with something to interest every child.

Learning to Read, Step by Step!

Ready to Read   Preschool–Kindergarten
• big type and easy words • rhyme and rhythm • picture clues
For children who know the alphabet and are eager to begin reading.

Reading with Help   Preschool–Grade 1
• basic vocabulary • short sentences • simple stories
For children who recognize familiar words and sound out new words with help.

Reading on Your Own   Grades 1–3
• engaging characters • easy-to-follow plots • popular topics
For children who are ready to read on their own.

Reading Paragraphs   Grades 2–3
• challenging vocabulary • short paragraphs • exciting stories
For newly independent readers who read simple sentences with confidence.

Ready for Chapters   Grades 2–4
• chapters • longer paragraphs • full-color art
For children who want to take the plunge into chapter books but still like colorful pictures.

STEP INTO READING® is designed to give every child a successful reading experience. The grade levels are only guides; children will progress through the steps at their own speed, developing confidence in their reading.

Remember, a lifetime love of reading starts with a single step!

Step into Reading, Random House, and the Random House colophon are registered trademarks of Penguin Random House LLC.

Visit us on the Web!
StepIntoReading.com
rhcbooks.com

Educators and librarians, for a variety of teaching tools, visit us at RHTeachersLibrarians.com

ISBN 978-0-7364-4296-1 (trade) — ISBN 978-0-7364-9025-2 (lib. bdg.)
ISBN 978-0-7364-4297-8 (ebook)

Printed in the United States of America

10 9 8 7 6 5 4 3 2 1

Mission: Teamwork

adapted by Natasha Bouchard

illustrated by the Disney Storybook Art Team

Random House 🏠 New York

This is Buzz Lightyear.

He is a Space Ranger.

Space Rangers
protect the galaxy.

Sox is a robot cat.

He makes a fuel crystal

for Buzz's spaceship.

Sox and Buzz
test the crystal.
It works!

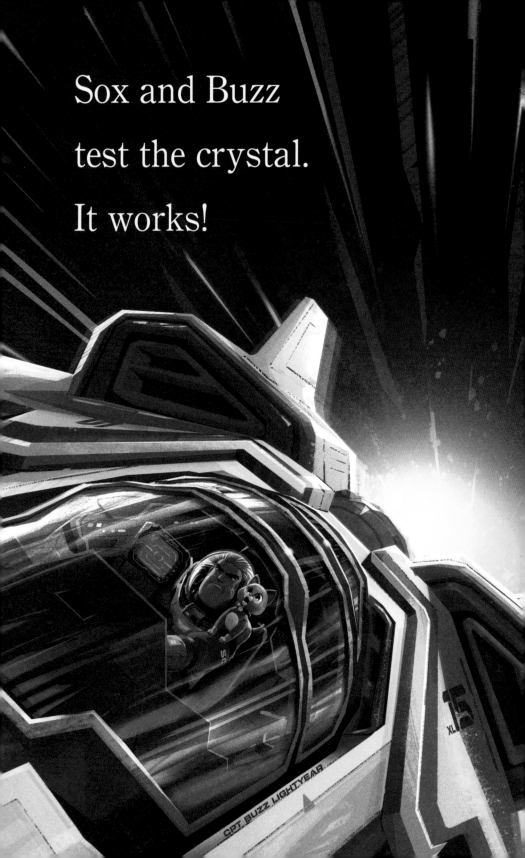

This is Zurg.

Zurg is the leader
of an alien robot army.

Zurg wants the crystal.

Zurg sends his
alien robot army
to find Buzz
and take the crystal.

This is Izzy.

Her dream is to be

a Space Ranger.

Izzy pushes Buzz
to the ground.
She hides Buzz
from an alien robot.

Soon another alien robot
finds Buzz.

Izzy's friends Mo and
Darby help fight it.

Mo aims and misses.
Then he strikes the
alien robot with a harpoon.
The alien is defeated.

Izzy, Mo, and Darby
are not Space Rangers.
But Buzz takes a chance
and makes them his team.

They will all stop Zurg
and protect the galaxy!

The new team flies
in a ship.

Zurg's ship chases them!

Zurg catches Buzz.

He takes Buzz
to his ship.

Buzz must escape!

He fights Zurg.

Then Buzz sees Izzy.

His friends are here

to rescue him!

Izzy throws Buzz

his wrist blaster.

Buzz fires at Zurg
outside a spaceship.
Zurg is defeated!

Oh, no!
The team's ship
is about to crash.
With Buzz's help,
they land the ship!

Together, this team

can complete any mission!